RUSS THOMPSON

KNOCKED DOWN

Finding Forward

Books

Published by Finding Forward Books
P.O. Box 8182, Long Beach, CA 90808
www.findingforwardbooks.com.

Editing by Laura Perkins. Series concept by
Pam Sheppard. Text set in Open Dyslexic Mono.

ISBN: 979-8-5279689-9-6 (Amazon paperback)
ISBN: 978-1-7373157-3-5 (Ingram paperback)
FILE: FF005-17G-2024-08-05

Summary: Tennison Sanders is a gifted high-
school football player with a chance to make
it in the pros someday. But he brings himself
down by making bad decisions. Follow him as he
learns the importance of teamwork, honesty,
and sacrifice.

BISAC Subject Codes: YOUNG ADULT FICTION /
Social Themes / Values and Virtues | YOUNG
ADULT FICTION / Sports and Recreation /
Football | YOUNG ADULT FICTION / Loners and
Outcasts

Lexile measure: HL400L

For Betty Jean,
our kids,
and grandkids.

CONTENTS

1 JUST WON'T

TUESDAY. History. Mr. Rubio hands back our papers from last week.

"Tennison, you need to get serious," he says. "This was almost a D."

The grade he gave me is a C. It could be better. But as long as I get a C on my grade check for football, that's good enough.

I'm the number one receiver in the Empire League. That's where my future is, football.

I had seven catches against Grant

Last week. Two of them were for touchdowns.

That's why we won. We won because of me.

To be a good receiver, you have to believe you will catch every ball that comes to you.

That's how it is for me. If I can touch it, I can catch it. I also have the speed. And I know how to be tricky and get open.

Coach Parra says I'm a natural. He was an all-pro receiver in Canada for the Winnipeg Blue Bombers, so he should know.

First, I'll get a scholarship to a major college. I already have scouts looking at me, so it shouldn't be too hard.

After that, with my talent, I think I can get drafted after my second year.

I'll be playing in the pros. I'll be famous. And I'll be making big money.

Mr. Rubio comes to the front of the classroom. He has a look on his face like he's mad about something.

"I stayed up late reading your reports last night," he says. "Some of them seemed like they might have been copied."

He looks around the room. His eyes stop at me.

I give him my honest look. His eyes move on.

"When you copy, it's called plagiarism," he says. "I found a website this morning that checks for it. I'll be using it from now on. If I catch you copying, you will get a NoPass."

The way he says it worries me. My report was on John Hancock. I copied some of it from a website I found.

I'll have to be more careful next time.

"You have to ask yourself two things," Mr. Rubio says. "First, how do you feel about lying? Second, how far will you go in life by cutting corners and not doing the work?"

The way I feel about lying, is that I only do it when I have to.

When it comes to cutting corners, I would never do it in football.

That would be stupid.

AFTER SCHOOL. Locker room. Practice starts in five minutes.

I sit on the bench in front of my locker and pull my jersey over my shoulder pads.

That's when I see them. Chuck left his shoes out.

He has Air Pros, size ten, the same size as me. They cost a lot of money.

Chuck is smart in school. But he's only a second-team running back.

He's also one of those rich kids who has everything.

I look down at my own shoes, cheap knockoffs from Price Mart.

The locker room is almost empty. Nobody will see me.

I pick up Chuck's shoes, put them in my locker, and click the lock shut.

I just won't be able to wear them to school for a while.

2 TOO LATE NOW

TWENTY MINUTES LATER. Football
field. We sit in the endzone and
stretch.

Coach Parra walks up and down the
rows. His face is wrinkled. And he
limps now. But I'm sure he used to
be fast.

"Football is a game you cannot
play halfway," he says. "It's a game
where you have to do everything you
can to win, not just some of the
things."

Everything he says is right. You

can't hold back. You have to go all the way.

"It's also about being a team," Coach Parra says. "It's about being there for the guy next to you. We have a tough game against Monroe this week. But by working hard and giving everything for each other, we can win."

I feel a little bad about taking Chuck's shoes, but not too bad. He shouldn't have left them out.

And when it comes to teamwork, we wouldn't have won last week without the seven catches I made.

We finish stretching and move to our groups. I go with the receivers for passing drills.

Diego comes to the line. He's a senior this year, probably the best quarterback in the league.

"Eagle-678," he says. "Hut!"

I run straight and angle left to the goal post.

Diego throws.

I lock my eyes on the ball, watch it all the way to my hands, and feel it with my fingertips.

It's all about concentration. And I have it. That's why I catch everything that comes to me.

We take turns getting the ball thrown to us.

Fifteen minutes later, Coach Parra blows his whistle. "Twenty plays," he says. "Full hitting."

The first one is a Mustang-242, a running play up the middle with Leo getting the ball.

"Hut!"

Leo blasts straight ahead and gets six yards. He's like a

bulldozer.

The next play is an Eagle-629, a
pass play.

"Hut!"

I fake to the left and sprint up
the sideline.

Diego throws. I catch the ball
and run to the endzone without
anyone touching me.

"Ten Cent, good job," Coach Parra
says.

I like that nickname, Ten Cent.
It will set me apart when I make it
to the pros.

LOCKER ROOM. I put on my shirt.

Chuck sits next to me. "Ten Cent,
have you seen my shoes?"

I look at the floor. I don't want
him to see my eyes. "What do you
mean?"

"Somebody took my Air Pros."

"Are you sure?"

He slams his locker and bangs his fist on it. "Somebody on this team stole my shoes!"

Maybe I shouldn't have taken them.

But there's no way he'll ever know it was me.

HOME. I walk in the front door. Grandpa stirs chili on the stove.

I put down my backpack. "Smells great."

He looks up. "You're late. We'll be eating in five minutes."

"Where's Mom?" I ask.

"Still at work."

It's been hard. The rent on our apartment went up, so we had to move in with Grandpa last month.

Mom works extra as much as she can, to save money.

I go to my room, close the door, and hide Chuck's shoes on the top shelf of the closet.

Grandpa is nosey. But I'm pretty sure he won't look there.

Dinner is ready when I come back to the kitchen.

Grandpa dishes out the chili from the stove. "Tennison, how was school?"

"I had a good practice. We play Monroe this week."

"I wasn't asking about football," he says. "How were your classes?"

"Fine."

"I didn't see you doing any homework last night."

"I didn't have any. I finished it at school."

"I know football is important to you," he says. "And I had fun when I played. But your classes are more important. Don't cut corners and make the same mistakes I made."

He's always bugging me about homework.

He won't be doing it when I make it to the pros.

EVENING. I sit at the kitchen table and open my laptop. It's held together with duct tape, so I have to be careful.

I get on the website for science. We have a test tomorrow on electricity.

It's hard to understand. I'm glad I sit next to Chuck.

One of the things I know about electricity, is that electric cars are fast. The Tesla Model S can go zero to sixty in less than three seconds.

They cost a lot. But when I make it to the pros, I'll be able to buy any car I want.

I think about Chuck's shoes in my closet.

Maybe I shouldn't have taken them, especially since I copy off him.

But it's too late now.

3   BEST RECEIVER

WEDNESDAY MORNING. Breakfast. I sit at the kitchen table eating cereal.

The game this Friday is a big one.

There were scouts from Colorado State and Arizona looking at me last week.

I'm sure there will be scouts again this week.

Mom comes in and sits across from me. She looks tired again.

"How was work last night?" I ask.

"I had to stay late because there

was a problem with getting the shelves stocked."

"Wasn't it better at Office Club?"

"In a way," she says. "But Price Mart will be better in the long run."

"Why is that?"

"They pay for your school if you take college classes. I can go at night and get a business degree."

"What will that do?"

"I'll have a better chance to get promoted," she says. "I can become a manager."

"I thought you already went to college."

"I did. But I never graduated."

"How come?"

"Things happened," she says. "That's what you have going for you with football. You can get a free college education."

"But once I get to the pros, it won't matter. I'll be making all kinds of money, anyway."

"What if you get hurt?"

"That's not going to happen. I know how to relax after I catch the ball. The guys who get hurt are the ones who fight it."

I can tell by the look on her face that she doesn't believe me.

But as soon as I get my first paycheck, I'm going to buy her a house.

SCIENCE. I sit next to Chuck. He has new shoes today, another pair of Air Pros.

I feel less bad about the shoes I stole yesterday.

I reach out my arm. Chuck gives me a fist bump.

"Ten Cent, good luck," he says.

"Thanks."

Ms. Wilcher comes to the front of the classroom with the tests in her hand. "There are fifteen multiple-choice questions and two essays. No talking. Keep your eyes on your own paper."

I don't know the first answer. I look sideways at Chuck's test.

He writes a B. That's what I write.

I don't know the next answer, either.

I copy most of my answers from Chuck, but not all of them. It would be too easy to get caught if I did.

The essays are harder. I see what Chuck writes. But I don't copy it

exactly. I put as much as I can into
my own words.

Chuck smiles when he finishes the
last essay. He'll probably get an A.

I smile too. I know I'll get at
least a C.

AFTER SCHOOL. Football field. We run
passing patterns against the
defensive backs.

Diego calls the next play, an
Eagle-678.

My job is to line up on the right
and run a post pattern.

Allen, the defensive back, gets
into position across from me.

He's tense and tight. That's why
I know I can fake him. I know how to
stay loose and go.

"Hut!"

I run straight and angle left.

Allen can't stay with me.

Diego throws. The ball flies into my hands.

I run into the endzone.

The next play is a Falcon-264, a pass. My job is to run a hook pattern.

Allen lines up across from me. I know I can lose him again.

"Hut!"

I run straight and curl inside at the fifteen-yard line.

Diego throws. I catch the ball and run into the endzone with nobody around me.

We're a good pair. Diego is the best quarterback in the league. I'm the best receiver.

4 ALL OVER

THURSDAY MORNING. Edison High. I stand with the football guys in a circle by the front gate.

Diego speaks up. "Ten Cent, did you see the sports section? You're the top receiver in the league again."

"What about the guy from Monroe?" I ask.

"He's right behind you."

The bell rings. We bump fists and go. It's nice to be on top.

SCIENCE. Ms. Wilcher hands back our tests from yesterday.

I get a C. But there's a note telling me to see her after class.

I hope she doesn't think I was cheating. Chuck also gets a note to see her on his test.

The bell rings. We go to her desk. I get ready to put on my innocent act.

She looks hard at us. "When I checked your tests yesterday, the essays were very similar. Then I looked closer. The multiple-choice answers were also similar."

I'm glad I didn't copy Chuck exactly. I would have been caught for sure.

She looks hard at me. "If you copy, it's a NoPass."

She looks hard at Chuck. "It's

also a NoPass if you let somebody copy."

She looks hard at both of us. "You guys have a lot going for you. And you're both talented athletes. Don't throw it away."

It surprises me that she thinks Chuck is talented.

He's a good running back. But when it comes to talent, he's not even close to me.

I hope he doesn't figure out that I copied off him.

AFTER SCHOOL. Practice field. We stretch in the endzone.

Coach Parra walks up and down the rows. "You've been working hard in practice. But for some of you, I'm concerned about your grades. Football is important. But your grades are your future. I expect you to make the same effort in your classes that you make in football."

I've heard this speech a thousand times. He always talks about working hard in class.

Grades are important for the other guys. But for me, it's different. It's different because of my talent level.

I have one more year of high school and two years of college.

After that, I'll be living in a big house and making millions.

HOME. I walk in the front door and sit at the kitchen table. Grandpa is making tacos tonight.

He turns to me from the stove. "Tennison, I got a call from your science teacher. We had a good talk."

She's never called before. I should have been more careful when I copied off Chuck.

His eyes drill into me. "She told me your test was like the paper of a kid sitting next to you. What was that about?"

"She talked to both of us after class. I don't know what happened."

I can tell by the look on his face that he doesn't believe me.

"She gave me some of the questions," he says. "Question number one asked about batteries, and how chemical energy is converted into electrical energy. How does that happen?"

"Batteries have chemicals inside. That's how they make electricity."

"Can you give an example?"

"It's complicated. But it's because of the chemicals."

"Interesting," he says. "Question three was about geothermal energy. What is that?"

"It's when steam comes out of the earth."

"How does it work?"

"It's hard to explain. But they use it to run big powerplants."

"Interesting."

I know he doesn't believe me. But I'll never admit to what I did.

Once you admit something, it's all over.

5 WATCHING ME

FRIDAY MORNING. Science. I don't like my new seat. Ms. Wilcher moved me away from Chuck.

The guy sitting next to me is Brandon. He's not very smart, so it would be stupid to copy off him.

I'll have to start using a cheat sheet.

Class ends. I get my grade check from Ms. Wilcher. It's a C.

I only have one more class to worry about.

HISTORY. Mr. Rubio comes to the front of the classroom.

We're on the Revolutionary War. He thinks it's the greatest thing in the world. But it's boring to me.

He says we should care because that's how our country got started.

I care about our country. But the main thing is that I need a C on my grade check.

He brings it to my desk just before the bell rings.

It's a C. I'm relieved.

"Tennison, watch out," he says. "You're only three points away from a D."

The way he says it worries me.

AFTER SCHOOL. Gym. I turn in my grade check to Coach Parra and go to the weight room.

The team moms hand out dinners. They give us turkey sandwiches, fruit, and oatmeal cookies.

I grab my food and sit against the wall. Diego and Chuck sit next to me.

"Did you hear about Leo?" Diego asks me.

"What happened?"

"He got a D from Mr. Rubio. He's out for this week."

I try to keep a blank look on my face. The same thing that happened to Leo could happen to me.

"Who's going to be the fullback?" I ask.

"I am," Chuck says. "Coach Parra told me a little while ago."

This is not good. Chuck is nothing compared to Leo.

The other backs and receivers

come over and sit with us.

One of them is Ellis, the backup quarterback. He has the weakest arm I've ever seen.

Diego looks at us. "I'll be putting up the ball a lot," he says. "Things will be happening fast. Let me know if you can beat the guy across from you."

It's going to be a wide-open game. I should be able to get a lot of catches tonight.

SIX-FIFTEEN. Weight room. We sit on the floor, all forty of us. The game starts in forty-five minutes.

Coach Parra comes to the front. "This is it. Monroe has a strong team. But if we play our best, we can beat them."

Chuck sits next to me. His fists

are balled up. He's tense and tight.

"Relax and do your jobs," Coach Parra says. "Go all-out on every play. Hit hard and have fun."

Chuck jumps up and runs to the bathroom. He's probably going to throw up.

He's too nervous.

Not me. I'm going to stay loose, get open, and watch the ball fly into my hands.

SIX-THIRTY. Football stadium. We stretch in the endzone. Coach Parra walks up and down the rows.

I look into the stands. They're getting full.

I know Mom and Grandpa will be here. They never miss a game.

I wonder about Dad. He said he might be coming. But he hasn't been to a game yet.

I remember youth football. He came to all my games.

I was little back then. That's when they started calling me Ten Cent.

But I had great hands and could catch every ball that was thrown to me.

We finish stretching and go to our groups for warm-up drills.

This is it. I have to look good tonight.

Once the game starts, everyone will be watching me.

6 STUCK

FIRST QUARTER. I catch my first pass and go back to the line.

Their left cornerback can't stay with me. I'll be getting open all night.

The signal from the side is for a Falcon-284, another pass play.

"Hut!"

I fake right, cut left to the center of the field, and curl in.

Diego throws.

I lock my eyes on the ball, watch it to my hands, and feel it with my fingertips. I turn up the field and gain fifteen yards.

I feel great at first. But Diego is down when I get back to the line. He looks like he's been knocked out.

"Number 55 got him," Chuck says. "They hit head-on."

We stand back while the trainer works on Diego. It looks bad.

Finally, Diego sits up.

Two guys get under his shoulders and help him to the sidelines.

He can walk. But his legs look like rubber.

Ellis comes in. He tries to act calm. But he's tense and tight. I don't think he'll be throwing.

The first play is a Mustang-241, a running play with Chuck going to the right.

My job is to run straight and

block the safety to the outside.

"Hut!"

I hit the safety square in the chest and drive him back. Chuck gains four yards.

Second down. The next play is a Bronco-273. Chuck will get the ball again and run outside to the left.

"Hut!"

I block the safety hard and knock him down.

Chuck breaks free, cuts right, and runs to the endzone for a touchdown.

We kick the extra point and make it. We're ahead now, 7-3.

I'm glad we scored. But it should have been Diego throwing and me catching the ball.

I look at the sidelines. An old silver Honda pulls up on the track behind the bench.

Diego's dad gets out and helps him into the front seat.

I wonder if Diego has a concussion. If he does, he might be out for a long time.

THIRD QUARTER. We have a small lead, 14-10. Ellis still hasn't thrown any passes.

We go to the line. The play is a Bronco-261. Chuck will run to my side.

"Hut!"

I block the cornerback and knock him down. Chuck follows behind me for a gain of eight yards.

I go back to the line.

"Ten Cent," Chuck says. "Nice block."

He's probably going to gain a lot

of yards tonight.

It will be good for the team. But it will be bad for me.

LOCKER ROOM. The game is over. We won 21-17. Everyone is joking around and laughing.

I'm glad we won. But I only caught two passes.

Coach Parra stands in front of us. "Offense, good job on the running game. Defense, great job of holding them to two touchdowns."

Last week, he was talking about the passes I caught. This week, it's nothing.

Chuck smiles. He's happy because he was the star.

But it should have been me. I would have been catching the ball all night if Diego hadn't been hurt.

The cheering dies down. Coach Parra puts up his hand for us to get quiet.

"One more thing," he says. "I'm sorry to say that Diego got a concussion. They're keeping him overnight at the hospital. It's going to be a while before he comes back."

This is bad. Weak-arm Ellis is our quarterback now.

I'm the best receiver in the league.

And I'm stuck with a quarterback who can't throw.

7 CHANCES ARE GOOD

SUNDAY AFTERNOON. We sit at the kitchen table, eating lunch. Grandpa made soup, chicken gumbo.

I like his cooking. But I don't like staying here.

Mom says we'll get our own place as soon as she gets her credit cards paid off.

I hope it's soon. The thing about Grandpa, is that he's always getting on my case about school.

I get up to dish myself another bowl of soup.

Mom speaks up. "Tennison, who are you playing this week?"

"Kennedy. It's an away game."

"What about Diego?" she asks. "Is he okay?"

"He's fine," I say. "His dad called Coach Parra."

There's no way I would tell her the truth. It would scare her. She never wanted me to play football in the first place.

"By the way," Grandpa says. "How are your classes going? I didn't see you doing any homework yesterday."

I knew he was going to say something about school, especially in front of Mom.

"It's under control," I say. "I'm getting with Ellis this afternoon to catch some passes. I'll start on my homework as soon as I get back."

I meant to study yesterday, but I just didn't feel like it.

EDISON HIGH. I climb the fence to the practice field. Ellis is already there.

"Ten Cent," he says. "Thanks for coming out. Coach Parra told me to be ready to throw this week."

I'm glad Coach Parra wants us to throw the ball. But I don't think Ellis will be ready.

I don't think he'll ever be ready.

I run an out pattern. Ellis throws. The ball goes wide. I dive and make the catch anyway.

I run more patterns. The same thing happens. He throws over my head, at my feet, and wide.

We go for an hour. He doesn't get

better. It's a lost cause.

Diego was the best quarterback in the league. Now I'm with Ellis, the worst.

If I don't catch any more passes this year, the college scouts are going to forget about me.

And if I don't make it to a major college, there's no way I'll make it to the pros.

AFTER DINNER. I sit at the kitchen table and stare at the laptop.

Every time I do homework, I feel dumb.

Science is bad because I can't copy off Chuck anymore.

History is bad because Mr. Rubio is on to me.

I go to the history website and read the first half of the chapter about the Revolutionary War.

My report for this week is about Patrick Henry. I type his name into the computer. A lot of sites come up. He was a brave guy who gave speeches against England.

This time, I copy from three different websites, not just one. I also put in more of my own words.

Mr. Rubio does this thing on our homework where he only grades a few random papers. On the rest, he just gives checkmarks.

I know it's cheating.

But chances are good that he won't even read mine.

8 CAN'T THROW

MONDAY. History. Mr. Rubio stands at the door when I get there.

"Tennison," he says. "Nice job on Friday."

"Thanks, Mr. Rubio."

He goes to the games. But I don't think he knows much about football. He probably has no idea that Friday was a bad game for me.

Class starts. Mr. Rubio comes to the front of the room and begins collecting our reports.

"I'm looking forward to reading

your papers," he says. "The better you can write, the stronger your voice will be. It will help you in college. It will also help you in life."

He might be right. But I don't like writing. Luckily, with my talent in football, I won't need to be good at it anyway.

PRACTICE FIELD. It's offense against defense, full hitting. Ellis calls an Eagle-234, a pass play.

"Hut!"

I run straight and curl inside. Ellis throws behind me. The ball hits the ground.

We go back to the line. Ellis looks at me like he's sorry.

The next play is a Falcon-648. Good, another pass play.

"Hut!"

I run straight and angle left to the goal post. Ellis throws the ball. This time, it's too high.

I go back to the line. Ellis looks at me again like he's sorry.

I don't care if he's sorry. I'm tired of it.

The next play is a Mustang-241, with Chuck running up the middle.

"Hut!"

Chuck breaks through and gains ten yards.

The next play is a Bronco-274, another running play.

"Hut!"

Chuck gains fifteen yards.

We're a running team now.

My season is over until Diego comes back.

ENDZONE. We finish running sprints and take a knee.

Coach Parra stands in front of us. "Football is much more than just a game," he says. "It's like life. And things go wrong, just like they do in life."

He's right. Things have gone very wrong. Ellis can't throw. And the college scouts are going to forget about me.

"The question is this," Coach Parra says. "What will you do when things get bad? Are you going to feel sorry for yourself and give up? Or are you going to come back harder with everything you have?"

How am I supposed to come back harder when Ellis can't even get the ball close to me?

HOME. After dinner. I go into my room, shut the door, and take Chuck's shoes out of the closet.

I finally know what to do with them.

I pull out the orange laces and replace them with the black ones from the shoes I'm wearing now.

I draw over the orange stripes with a black marking pen. The orange is hard to cover, so it takes me three times.

But they look good when I'm done. It's nice to have new shoes to wear. And Chuck will never know they're his.

I remember eight years ago, when Mom and Dad were still married.

There was plenty of money back then. We even used to go on vacations.

But now that they're divorced, we're broke all the time.

I'll be glad when I make it to the pros. I'll be able to buy all the shoes I want.

Then I remember. Ellis can't throw.

9 DON'T HAVE

TUESDAY MORNING. Breakfast. Grandpa stands at the stove. He's cooking scrambled eggs and bacon.

I think about school. We're having another test in science today.

I have to get a good grade without copying off Chuck.

I pull out the cheat sheet I made. The writing is small, but I can read it. The sheet folds up and fits into the palm of my hand.

Grandpa turns sideways from the

stove. I slide the cheat sheet into my pocket.

"Tennison, what's that?" he asks.

"Nothing."

"What did you just put in your pocket?"

I pull out my pen and click it. "I guess it was this."

"Did you study for your science test?" he asks.

"Yep. I spent two hours."

"Good," he says. "The harder you work, the farther you'll go."

NEPTUNE STREET. I walk to school and look down at my new shoes.

They feel good. I've always wanted Air Pros. Nobody will know they're stolen.

I reach the gray house on the corner. The sprinklers come on.

I walk quickly. But my shoes get wet.

Some of the orange shows through where I covered it with the marker last night.

I can't go back home to change shoes, or Grandpa will ask questions.

I'll have to be careful not to get any more water on them.

SCIENCE. Ms. Wilcher comes to the front of the classroom.

"Clear your desks," she says. "Keep your eyes on your own papers. There will be twenty multiple-choice questions and two essays."

She passes out the tests. I try not to be nervous. I slide my cheat sheet out of my pocket and hide it in my hand.

I don't know the answer to the first question. But I find it on the cheat sheet and mark a C on my test paper.

I do the same for the next question, and the next.

I get to question twenty, open my hand to look at the cheat sheet, and write a D for the answer.

Someone comes up behind me. I turn my head. It's Ms. Wilcher.

She bends down and writes NoPass on my test paper.

This is bad. I should have been more careful.

What if I don't get a C on the grade check this week?

LOCKER ROOM. Practice starts in twenty minutes.

I sit in front of my locker and

Look down. More of the orange on my shoes is showing.

Chuck isn't here yet. I have to move fast.

I untie my left shoe, put it in my locker, and begin taking off my right.

Somebody comes up behind me.

"Ten Cent," Chuck says. "How's it going?" He opens his locker and sits next to me.

I cross my right shoe under my left foot to hide it.

"Got some new shoes?" Chuck asks.

"Not really. I just never wore them to school before."

"How are they?" he asks.

"Fine."

"Mind if I look?"

There's nothing I can do. I take off my right shoe and give it to him.

He rubs one of the stripes with his thumb. More of the black comes off.

He looks under the tongue. His face gets hard. "I wonder how my name got here?"

I take a deep breath. What if he tells the guys?

"How much did they cost?" I ask.

He looks me in the eye. "Ninety-four."

"You'll have it tomorrow."

I stare straight ahead as we finish dressing. Nothing more is said.

I don't have the money.

10   SHOULD BE ENOUGH

PRACTICE IS OVER. I sit across from my locker and get dressed.

Chuck sits next to me. He says nothing. He doesn't even say thanks for blocking for him.

Two weeks ago, I was the star of the team. Now, I'm a blocker. And Chuck knows I stole from him.

I don't know where I'm going to get his ninety-four dollars.

And I don't know what to do about science.

HOME. I open the top drawer of my dresser, take out my money, and count it.

Forty-seven dollars. That's all I have. How am I going to pay Chuck?

I get an idea and go to the kitchen. Grandpa is getting dinner ready.

I go to the sink and pour a glass of water. "It was sad at school today."

"What happened?" he asks.

"The principal made an announcement this morning. A kid died of cancer. He was in three of my classes."

"I'm sorry to hear that."

"The school is doing a fundraiser to help the family pay for the funeral."

I can tell by Grandpa's face that

he believes me.

He pulls out his wallet and gives me twenty dollars. "Tennison, this is for the fundraiser. We know what it feels like."

It was two years ago when Grandma died. She had been sick for a long time. We're still hurting.

I feel bad about lying to Grandpa. But I don't have a choice.

I put the money in my pocket and sneak into Mom's room.

She keeps cash in the bottom drawer of her nightstand. She calls it her crazy cash.

I count the bills, ninety dollars. I take thirty and put it into my pocket with the money I got from Grandpa.

This is the first time I've taken more than a few dollars from her.

I know it's wrong. But I'll never
do it again.

EVENING. I sit at the kitchen table
with the laptop.

It bugs me to look at the duct
tape. But I'll be able to buy a new
laptop every week when I make it to
the pros.

I begin working on an apology
letter to Ms. Wilcher.

I have to make her feel sorry for
me. It's my only chance to play.

Dear Ms. Wilcher,
    I am very sorry for copying on
the test today. I know it was wrong.
    Things have been bad at home. My
grandma died of cancer. And my mom
had to get a new job.
    We got kicked out of our

apartment. We don't have a regular place to live anymore, so we stay with my grandpa.

He's very sick. I have to take care of him and do all the cooking. Sometimes, when I try to study, I can't think.

Please give me another chance. I promise I will never copy again.

If I don't get at least a C on my grade check this week, I won't be able to play in the game on Friday.

Sincerely,
Tennison Sanders

I know I shouldn't lie. But after this week, I'll never do it again.

I go back to the chapter and do three extra-credit assignments. It should be enough to bring my grade back up to a C.

11   USED TO BE

WEDNESDAY MORNING. Science. I put my apology letter on Ms. Wilcher's desk.

I'm pretty sure the letter will make her feel sorry for me. And with the extra credit I did, I should be able to keep my C.

From this point on, I'll never copy on a test again.

I think about football. If things work out, this Friday will be the last game for Ellis.

When Diego comes back, we'll

still have three games left in the season.

It should be enough time for me to get my catches up.

Ms. Wilcher asks me to stay after class when the bell rings.

"Tennison, thanks for your letter," she says. "I'm sorry things have been rough for you at home."

"That's okay. We're making it. I really am sorry for what I did. I'll never do it again."

She smiles. "I'm glad you also did the extra credit. I'll check it tonight."

I think she believes me. I'm glad I wrote the apology letter, even if a lot of it wasn't true.

LOCKER ROOM. Practice starts soon. Chuck sits next to me.

I take the ninety-four dollars out of my pocket and put it on the bench next to him.

He picks up the money. "Ten Cent, thanks."

"Are we straight now?" I ask.

"Yep, we're straight."

"I hope you don't say anything to the guys."

He puts the money in his pocket. "Don't worry. I wasn't planning to."

Chuck is a nice guy. If he had stolen from me, I think I would have done something.

PRACTICE FIELD. It's offense against defense, full hitting.

The next play is an Eagle-249, a pass play.

"Hut!"

I fake left and run up the

sideline. Ellis throws.

The ball is on target and flies into my hands.

It feels good to run across the goal line. Things are getting better.

The next play is a Mustang-283.

Chuck will get the ball and run to the right.

My job is to block the outside linebacker.

"Hut!"

I blast the linebacker and knock him down. Chuck gains fifteen yards.

"Way to go!" Coach Parra yells. "That's what we need on Friday!"

The hit felt good. But I would rather catch the ball.

NEPTUNE STREET. I walk home. The sprinklers come on again at the gray house on the corner.

My shoes get wet. But these are my own, so it doesn't matter.

Things are looking up.

Chuck didn't tell anybody that I stole from him. And I should be getting a C from Ms. Wilcher.

It's just like Coach Parra says. When things go bad, you have to keep trying.

When Diego comes back, I'll be catching the ball again.

Everything will be back the way it used to be.

12 WON'T BE PLAYING

THURSDAY MORNING. Diego stands with us in our circle by the front gate.

"How's your head?" Chuck asks him.

"I was hoping to get smarter," Diego says. "But here I am back with you guys."

Everybody laughs. It's a relief to have him back. I'll be catching the ball again.

"When do you get to play?" I ask.

"Maybe next week," he says. "I have to get cleared by the doctor."

From the way he sounds, I'm sure he'll be okay.

Things are looking up.

HISTORY. Mr. Rubio frowns when he returns my Patrick Henry report.

It's a NoPass. He also wrote a comment:

Copied from history.com/patrick-henry. See me after class.

The game is tomorrow. What if he gives me less than a C on my grade check?

The bell rings. I go back to his desk.

"Tennison, you heard what I said to the class about copying. Why did you do it?"

"I don't know."

"It's your life," he says. "And the things you do are your choice. If you choose to work hard, you can go far in life. If you choose to cheat, sooner or later it comes back on you."

Everything is falling apart. I have to do something.

LUNCH. I sit with the guys and try to act normal. What do I do about history?

The bell rings. I leave the food court.

Diego walks up next to me. "Ten Cent, I couldn't tell you this in front of the other guys. But I might not be back for the rest of the season."

"What are you talking about?"

"I had a stage three concussion,

the worst there is. My head wouldn't stop spinning. And I was throwing up."

"I thought you said you were going back to the doctor."

"I am. But she might not clear me."

Diego says more. But I don't hear any of it. If he doesn't come back, my season is over.

HOME. I open the front door. Grandpa is speaking on his phone.

"I'm sorry it happened," he says. "Thanks for letting me know. I'll talk to his mom when she gets home tonight."

I have a feeling it's Mr. Rubio. I go to my room before Grandpa can say anything.

DINNER. Mom had to work late, so it's just Grandpa and me.

We sit down to eat. I know I'm in trouble.

"I got a call from Mr. Rubio," he says. "He told me you copied from the Internet."

I look down at my plate. I can't look him in the eye.

"I'm not perfect," Grandpa says. "I've made a lot of mistakes in my life. But I finally learned I had to do things the right way. And I learned I had to tell the truth."

I didn't expect this. He's speaking to me like I'm an adult.

He looks me in the eye. "You can choose to be honest and work hard. Or you can choose to go the other way. It's your life. It will be what you make of it."

I was ready for him to yell at
me.

This is worse.

MIDNIGHT. I finish my new report on
Patrick Henry for Mr. Rubio's class.

It took me four hours. I looked
up five different websites and wrote
everything in my own words. I made
it six pages long to make up for the
copying I did. It's the best report
I've ever done.

It's my only chance to bring up
my grade in history.

If it doesn't work, I won't be
playing in the game tomorrow night.

13 WON'T BE ABLE

FRIDAY MORNING. I walk to school down Neptune Street.

Normally, I would be excited about the game tonight. But not today.

If I don't get good grades from Ms. Wilcher and Mr. Rubio, I'm out.

SCIENCE. Class begins. Ms. Wilcher talks about chemical energy.

I don't hear any of it. All I can think about is my grade.

The bell rings. Class ends. I go

back to her desk.

She smiles when she gives me my grade check. It's a C.

"Tennison, good luck in the game tonight," she says. "I know it's important to you."

It's a relief. But I still have one more class to worry about.

HISTORY. I try not to be nervous. But my hand shakes when I give Mr. Rubio my report on Patrick Henry.

"I'm sorry again for copying," I say. "This one is done right. And I wrote six pages."

"I'll take a look at it," he says. "But don't get your hopes up."

Class begins. I can't think. Everything is a blur.

I go to Mr. Rubio's desk when the bell rings.

He has a hard look on his face. "Tennison, I skimmed your report. It looks like you did a good job. But it doesn't make up for how you copied the first time. I'll read it carefully and add it to your grade for next week. But for this week, you're going to have to take the consequences for what you did."

He gives me my grade check.

It's a D.

I feel numb.

LUNCH. I sit with the guys and try to act like nothing is wrong.

But I won't be playing tonight. I'll be off the team.

What do I do?

PERIOD FIVE ENDS. The bell rings. Football is next.

I walk down the hallway and get to the bottom of the stairs.

How will I face Coach Parra? How will I face the guys?

I have to do something.

I begin limping and go to the health office. I sit down like I'm hurt.

"What happened?" the nurse asks.

"It's my ankle. I fell when I was coming down the stairs."

"I don't see any swelling," she says. "How did you fall?"

"A girl in front of me tripped. When I tried to help her, I fell and twisted my ankle."

The nurse has a look on her face like she doesn't believe me. I have to try harder.

"I twisted it bad," I say. "I felt it pop. It really hurts."

She touches my ankle again. I close my eyes to act like I'm in pain.

"I think you need to see a doctor," she says. "Can somebody pick you up?"

"My grandpa can come and get me. Could you send a note to Coach Parra? I won't be able to play in the game tonight."

14 HURTING

URGENT CARE. I sit with Grandpa in the waiting room.

I can tell he's worried about me. I know it was wrong to lie. But I had to do it.

They call my name. We walk through a door and down a hallway to an exam room.

I limp to make it look like I'm really hurt.

Ten minutes pass. The doctor comes in. She doesn't smile and has a serious look on her face. It's going to be hard to fool her.

She moves my foot around. I act like it hurts.

She watches as I take a few steps. I act like the pain is killing me.

"Usually with an injury like this, there's swelling and bruising," she says. "But I don't see any. On a scale of one to ten, how bad is the pain?"

"About a nine."

"Let's have you go across the hall for an X-ray."

I think I fooled her.

But what's going to happen when she sees the X-ray?

HOME. I lie on the couch with a bag of ice on my ankle.

Mom comes into the living room.

"Grandpa told me what happened. He said you were in a lot of pain. I'm glad it's not broken."

"Me too."

She looks hard at me. "I wonder why there's no swelling."

"I don't know. But I think the ice is working."

"You seem to be hurting a lot. I wonder why the doctor didn't give you any pain medication."

"I guess I don't need any."

"By the way," she says. "How was your grade check?"

"It was fine."

"Do you have it?"

"I think I dropped it when I fell on the stairs."

"That's too bad," she says. "Did you happen to need thirty dollars for anything?"

"No, not at all."

"Interesting," she says. "I thought I had more money in my crazy cash."

This is bad. She doesn't believe me.

EVENING. I pretend to sleep on the couch. Mom and Grandpa talk in the kitchen.

"I don't know what to do," Mom says. "Tennison is lying to us."

"I know," Grandpa says. "There's nothing wrong with his ankle."

"I bet he got a D on his grade check," Mom says. "I asked him about it, and he said he lost it."

"Mr. Rubio told me he was cheating," Grandpa says. "He's probably the one who gave it to him."

"And I'm pretty sure he stole thirty dollars from my crazy cash. I noticed it was gone this afternoon."

"That reminds me," Grandpa says. "I gave him twenty dollars the other day. He said there was a fundraiser at school for a kid who died of cancer. I bet he was lying about that, too."

"I don't know what to do," Mom says. "He's getting more and more like his dad."

Her words feel like a slap.

Dad has always had a lie for everything.

I roll over on the couch and moan to act like I'm hurting.

15 HOW WILL

SATURDAY MORNING. The sun shines
through my window.

I'm wide awake. But I don't want
to get up.

I hear voices from the kitchen.
Mom and Grandpa are probably making
breakfast burritos.

They're my favorite. But I don't
want to go out there. I don't want
to face them.

It hit me last night when Mom
said I was turning out like Dad. I
always promised myself I would never

be like him.

Mom calls out from the kitchen.
"Tennison, breakfast!"

I say nothing. Maybe she'll think
I'm asleep.

Steps come down the hall.

"Tennison, we have breakfast
ready."

"Okay."

I get out of bed and get dressed.

I don't know what I'll say to
them. But I'm tired of lying.

I open the door and walk to the
kitchen.

I don't limp.

BREAKFAST. I finish my first
burrito. Mom and Grandpa haven't
said anything yet.

I start on my second one. Maybe
they're going to talk to me later.

"Your ankle looked better when you walked to the table," Mom says.

This is it. I look straight at her. "That's because it wasn't hurt in the first place."

Her eyebrows raise. But she doesn't say anything.

Grandpa looks me in the eye. "What happened?"

I can't hold back. It all comes out.

I tell about the lies, the cheating, the shoes I stole, and the money I stole.

I feel drained when I'm done.

But I also feel better.

AFTER BREAKFAST. I stand at the sink washing dishes. Mom dries. Grandpa puts them away.

I feel lighter now, like a load

has been lifted off my shoulders.

"There was no excuse for what you did," Mom says. "But you've done the right thing by admitting it. You've taken the first step toward getting yourself right."

"Thanks."

"What are you going to do next?" Grandpa asks.

"I guess I'm going to quit lying and start doing the work in my classes."

"That's good," he says. "What about football?"

"I guess I need to talk to Coach Parra. He'll probably kick me off the team."

"That's what my coach would have done," Grandpa says. "But maybe he'll let you back. If he does, you have to show you're playing for the team, not yourself."

"There's another thing," Mom says. "Everybody at school probably thinks of you as a liar. You thought you were fooling them. But I bet you weren't. You have to figure out what you're going to do about that."

She's right. I have a lot to figure out.

What will I do on Monday?

How will I face Coach Parra?

How will I face the guys?

16 MAYBE

MONDAY MORNING. School starts in thirty minutes. I knock on the door of Coach Parra's office.

He looks up from his desk and waves me in.

I sit in the chair across from him. I can tell he's mad at me because of Friday.

I don't want to do this. But I have to.

"We missed you at the game," he says. "How's your ankle?"

My right heel taps on the floor.

I push down on my leg to stop it. "My ankle is fine. There was nothing wrong with it."

His stare cuts into me.

I confess everything. I tell him about the lying and cheating. I admit to stealing Chuck's shoes. It all comes out.

Football is over for me now. But at least I'm being honest.

"Tennison, there is no excuse for what you did," he says. "But it's good that you're telling the truth now. Of course, you'll have to earn your way back onto the team."

I never thought he would say that. I didn't think I would get a second chance.

"First, you need to get your grades up," he says. "You have to get a good grade check on Friday.

You also have to prove yourself to the guys. They need to know that you're sorry for what you did. And they need to know that you're playing for the team now, not just yourself."

The bell rings. I leave for first period.

I know what I have to do. It's going to be the hardest thing I've ever done.

FOOTBALL FIELD. We stretch in the endzone. Nobody jokes around because we lost the game on Friday.

I feel the guys looking at me. But nobody has said anything. I try not to show how nervous I am.

Coach Parra stands in front of us. I tell myself to be calm.

"Tennison came to me this

morning," he says. "We had a talk. He has some things he wants to say to you."

He's always called me Ten Cent. But not now.

I don't deserve it.

I walk to the front and force myself to face them. "There was nothing wrong with my ankle on Friday. I got a D on my grade check in history. It happened because I turned in a report that I copied off the Internet. I faked getting hurt because I didn't want to face you."

Most of them look down. Some of them look up at me. I wish I knew what they were thinking.

There's more I have to say. "The other thing I need to tell you, is that I'm the one who stole Chuck's shoes. I know it was wrong. And I apologize. When it came to playing on this team, all I cared about was myself. I just wanted to catch passes and be a star. I feel terrible for what I did."

Nobody makes a sound.

I'm drained.

PRACTICE. I stand on the sidelines with the rest of the second team. The first team is out there, running plays.

My replacement, Rocky, catches everything that comes to him. I didn't know he was so good. Maybe I'm not so great after all.

"Second team," Coach Parra says. "Get in there."

The first play is a Bronco-281. My job is to block the cornerback.

"Hut!"

I knock him hard to the outside. The halfback turns inside and runs to the goal line.

The next play is a Mustang-262.

"Hut!"

I blast into the safety and drive him backward. We gain ten yards.

We do five more running plays. I hit hard on all of them.

My days of catching passes and being a star are over.

I'm a blocker now.

LOCKER ROOM. I lace up my old shoes. Chuck puts on his new Air Pros.

I wish he would say something. I click my locker shut.

"You had some nice blocks out there today," Chuck says. "And it took guts to admit what you did. I hope you get to play on Friday."

97

He looks me in the eye and puts his hand out.

We shake.

Maybe things are going to get better.

17 MAYBE I CAN

TUESDAY. History. I sit and wait for class to start. I feel like I've been kicked.

I wish I hadn't lied.

I wish I hadn't cheated.

I wish I could go back and change what I did.

When the season started, I was at the top. My grades were good enough. And I was the best receiver in the league.

But now, I'm not even starting.

And I won't even get a game

uniform this week unless I bring up my history grade.

The bell rings. Mr. Rubio comes to the front of the classroom. He has a serious look on his face.

"When I stand here and look at each of you, I don't just think about where you are right now," he says. "I think about where you will be ten years from now."

I used to be sure I would be playing pro football. I thought I would be making millions. Not anymore.

"When you go through life, you have choices," he says. "You can choose to be lazy and take shortcuts. Or you can choose to work hard and do things the right way. You can choose to be successful. Or you can choose to fail."

I think about what I did.
Everything he's saying is true.
Every mistake I made was my own
choice.

FOOTBALL PRACTICE. I stand on the
sidelines and watch the first team.
Rocky makes another catch.

He's the primary receiver now,
the new main guy.

He also has a great name, Rocky.
It's the kind of name people will
remember if he ever makes it big.

"Second team," Coach Parra says.
"Get in there."

The first play is a Falcon-749, a
pass.

"Hut!"

I fake left, run up the sideline,
and get open.

Ellis throws. It goes to the

tight end. He turns up the field and gains eight yards.

The next play is a Bronco-242. My job is to hit the middle linebacker. I knock him down, and the running back scores.

The play after that is a Mustang-281. I block hard on the safety, and we gain fifteen yards.

I don't think Ellis will be throwing to me.

I'm paying for the mistakes I made.

PRACTICE ENDS. The rest of the team goes into the locker room.

I walk to the goal line with Coach Parra.

"Is it manmakers?" I ask.

"Yep."

"How many?"

"Not sure," he says. "It depends on how you do."

He blows his whistle. I run forward.

He blows his whistle. I dive to the ground.

He blows his whistle. I get up and run again.

I run, dive, and get up every fifteen yards.

I reach the goal line and turn around. That's the first manmaker.

I look at Coach Parra and breathe hard to catch my breath.

"Not good enough," he says.

He blows his whistle again. I run again.

Down, up, run. Over and over.

By the tenth manmaker, I can barely stand.

"Tennison, that's it," Coach

Parra says. "Only two more days, and you're done."

It's a long walk back to the locker room.

But it's my own fault. It's the price I have to pay to get back on the team.

HOME. Eleven o'clock. I finish my report on Alexander Hamilton for Mr. Rubio's class.

It's two pages long. But it took me three hours to write it.

I feel good because I worked hard and did it right.

Maybe I can get an A.

18 FEEL GOOD

WEDNESDAY. History. Mr. Rubio comes to the front of the classroom.

"I decided to try something new," he says. "It's called mystery writer. I will collect your reports, shuffle them, and pick three to read out loud. I will not tell you the names of the people who wrote them."

I don't like this. What if he picks mine?

The first report is about John Adams, the second president of the United States. Everybody claps when

Mr. Rubio finishes reading.

The next paper is about King George III. He was the King of England during the Revolutionary War. Everybody claps for that paper, too.

Mr. Rubio shuffles the papers again. "This next report is about Alexander Hamilton. He was a key figure and played a very important role in the founding of our country."

He reads my report. I don't want to hear it. I put my head down.

The people in the class clap louder for my report than the other two.

I smile inside.

FOOTBALL PRACTICE. I stand on the sidelines with the rest of the second team.

The first team runs a Mustang-242. Chuck blasts up the middle and gains four yards. I didn't know he had so much power.

The next play is a pass, an Eagle-349.

Rocky dives for the ball and catches it with his fingertips. He makes it look easy. I wish it was me out there.

"Second team," Coach Parra says. "Your turn."

The first play is a run, a Bronco-264. I blast hard on the outside linebacker.

Leo gains six yards. I wonder if he'll get to play on Friday. His grades still aren't good enough, just like mine.

We run ten more plays. None of

them are passes. I hit hard on all
of them.

I feel good inside when I come
off the field.

I probably won't be playing on
Friday. But I made some tough blocks
today.

AFTER PRACTICE. I stand behind the
goal line and wait for Coach Parra
to start me on manmakers.

"Tennison, did you learn anything
yesterday?" he asks.

"I learned that I'm not as great
as I thought I was."

"What else?"

"I learned about telling the
truth and doing things right."

He blows his whistle.

I run.

He blows his whistle again.

I hit the ground.

He gives me eleven manmakers.

I'm dead when they're over. But I feel good about myself.

19   HARD SEASON

FRIDAY MORNING. The football guys stand in a circle by the front gate. Chuck makes room for me.

I smile and laugh at the jokes. But I don't say anything.

I don't belong yet.

HISTORY. Mr. Rubio gives me a C on my grade check.

"You turned things around," he says. "I'm proud of you."

He shakes my hand. I can tell by his grip that he means it.

After all this work, I'm back on the team.

PASSING PERIOD. I walk to lunch. Leo comes up next to me.

"Ten Cent, I made it," he says. "My grades are okay."

"That's great," I say. "Me too."

"Maybe you'll be blocking for me."

"That would be nice," I say. "But we probably won't be playing unless we get ahead by a big score."

FOOTBALL GAME. First quarter. Jefferson scores a touchdown. We're tied now, 7-7.

I don't like being on the sidelines. But at least I'm back on the team.

SECOND QUARTER. We score our second touchdown and go ahead 14-7.

Jefferson has a good team. It's going to be a close game.

Leo stands next to me. We both want to play. But I don't think it will happen.

THIRD QUARTER. Chuck runs into the endzone for another touchdown.

The score is 28-7. But Jefferson could still come back.

"What do you think?" Leo asks me. "I don't know. It's pretty tight."

FOURTH QUARTER. We're ahead, 35-7. There are three minutes left. We get the ball on the forty-yard line.

"Second team," Coach Parra says. "Get in there."

Leo and I run in. The first play

is a Bronco-221. It's a running play with Leo getting the ball.

"Hut!"

I cut inside and block the safety. We gain six yards.

The next play is a Mustang-263, a running play with Leo getting the ball again.

"Hut!"

I block the cornerback and knock him outside. Leo gains twelve yards.

Thirty seconds left.

The next play is a Mustang-282, a running play to the outside.

"Hut!"

I blast the defensive end and knock him down.

I hear cheering and look up. Leo crosses the goal line.

All I did was block. But I feel good when I run off the field.

"Ten Cent, great job," Coach Parra says. "You made a super hit on that defensive end."

I didn't think it would happen. He called me Ten Cent.

HOME. Mom and Grandpa are watching the news when I come in the door.

"Tennison, you had some nice blocks," Grandpa says.

I sit on the couch next to Mom. "Thanks. I didn't think I would like blocking. But I do."

"Some college scouts were sitting behind us," Mom says. "They were talking about you."

"What did they say?"

"They knew you could catch," Grandpa says. "But they couldn't believe it when they saw you block, especially when you blasted that defensive end."

It's been a hard season. Maybe I'm back. Maybe it's going to be okay.

20 LIKE THEM NOW

MONDAY MORNING. Science. Ms. Wilcher hands back our tests from Friday.

She smiles when she puts my paper on my desk.

It's a B.

I remember when I thought I had to cheat to get good grades.

Not anymore.

HISTORY. Mr. Rubio draws names for our report topics this week. Mine is Ben Franklin.

It's not due until Thursday. But

I'm going to start on it this evening.

I'm going to work hard and do it right.

LOCKER ROOM. I sit next to Chuck. Practice starts in twenty minutes.

He puts on his shoulder pads. "Ten Cent, did you see the new team chart?"

"No. What about it?"

"You're back on first team."

"Are you sure?" I ask.

"Very sure."

It's been a long way back. I made a lot of mistakes.

It wasn't fun getting knocked down.

But I got up again.

I take off my shoes and put them in my locker.

They're my knockoffs from Price Mart, the ones I hated.

They need new laces. And the soles are worn out.

But I came by them honestly.

I like them now.

ACKNOWLEDGMENTS

I would like to express my sincere gratitude to all of the people who gave me feedback while I was writing this book.

COFFEE HOUSE WRITERS GROUP: Elise Benevides, Christine Marie Bryant, Nicholas Chiazza, Robyn Dolan, Synida Fontes, Clyde Fugami, Avery Goodwin, Lois Ann Goossen, Anita Hamilton, Samantha Hancox-Li, Brenda Hill, Alex Khansa, Brandon Kuys, Darian Lane, Will Lee, Meng Lien, John Lowell, Martin Lowry, Tiffany Lum, Steve McCarthy, Christina Moria, Dollie Mason, Scott McClelland, Viet Nguyen, Jean Pliska, Yu Shen, Lorraine Silvers, Sara Skinner, Annick Tumolo, Emily

Wilder, AnneLise Wilhelmson, and Dennis Wolverton.

SOCIETY OF CHILDREN'S BOOK WRITERS AND ILLUSTRATORS: Tim Burke, Melanie Castillo, Jonathan Chew, Mandy Chew, Lisa Gold, Christine Jelbert, and Esther Tenenbaum.

SOUTHERN CALIFORNIA WRITERS CONFERENCE: Andrew Berkowitz, Gayle Carline, Kalie Cassidy, Greg Clumpner, Simone Fox, Emily Heebner, Jason Hook, Thomas Kennedy, Bethany Lopez, Jennifer Silva Redmond, Laura Taylor, Janis Thomas, Thomas Wing, and Claudia Whitsitt.

WRITERS INK: Tim Burke, Emily Heebner, Niki House, Kathleen Troy, Teri Vitters, and Eric Young.

Thank you, Pam Sheppard, for your advice on creating this series.

Thank you, Laura Perkins, for your careful editing and guidance.

Thank you, Betty Jean, for your patience, your suggestions, and for being my wife.

ABOUT THE AUTHOR

 My dream of becoming a writer started at Whitworth College. I was lucky to have a teacher, Dr. Tammy Reid, who believed in me and encouraged me. After college, I began a career as an educator, teaching reading and English at a middle school in Los Angeles. I went to college at night to earn a doctorate in education. I then served as a high-school principal and district administrator. One of the most important things I have learned is that everyone can achieve success. Set your sights high, work hard, and never give up. Strive to be the best that you can be.

FINDING FORWARD BOOKS

At Finding Forward Books, we publish easy-to-read novels with positive life lessons about teens overcoming challenges in their lives. Our goal is to help students improve their reading skills, develop positive attitudes, and increase their success in school.

The books are suitable for all students, including English learners and those with learning disabilities. Lexile measures range from 390 to 560.

The books have been praised in *Kirkus Reviews*, *Publishers Weekly BookLife Reviews*, *Foreword Clarion Reviews*, and *BlueInk Reviews*.

ADDITIONAL TITLES

TAKEN AWAY. A teen learns to cope after his dad is sent to prison.

NO PLACE TO HIDE. A discouraged teen improves his reading skills.

NEVER WANTED. A neglected teen is placed in a foster home.

ALL ALONE. A teen learns to deal with his mom's alcoholism.

TORN. A student with everything learns to care about another student who has nothing.

OVERSPRAY. A teen experiences grief after his father dies.

BLUE WALL. A troubled teen battles back from depression.

LETTERZ. A teen struggling with dyslexia learns how to succeed in school.

CANS. A teen who dreams of attending college struggles against poverty.

FINDING HOME. A homeless teen strives to find a better life.

Finding Forward Books
Easy-to-Read Novels with Positive
Life Lessons for Teens
www.findingforwardbooks.com